SOLON

ATHENIAN STATESMAN AND POET

Leaders of the Ancient World™

SOLON

ATHENIAN STATESMAN AND POET

BEATRIZ SANTILLIAN AND
BERNARD RANDALL

Rosen YA™
NEW YORK

Published in 2018 by The Rosen Publishing Group, Inc.
29 East 21st Street, New York, NY 10010

First Edition

Library of Congress Cataloging-in-Publication Data

Names: Santillian, Beatriz, author. | Randall, Bernard, co-author.
Title: Solon : Athenian statesman and poet / Beatriz Santillian and Bernard Randall.
Description: First edition. | New York : Rosen Publishing, 2018. | Series: Leaders of the ancient world | Audience: Grades 7–12. | Includes bibliographical references and index.
Identifiers: LCCN 2016053657 | ISBN 9781508174936 (library bound)
Subjects: LCSH: Solon, approximately 630 B.C.–approximately 560 B.C.—Juvenile literature. | Statesmen—Greece—Biography—Juvenile literature. | Poets, Greek—Biography—Juvenile literature. | Philosophers—Greece—Biography—Juvenile literature. | Athens (Greece)—Politics and government—Juvenile literature.
Classification: LCC DF224.S7 S26 2018 | DDC 938/.02092 [B]—dc23
LC record available at https://lccn.loc.gov/2016053657

Manufactured in the United States of America

On the cover: *Foreground*: A bust of Solon from the Naples National Archaeological Museum. *Background*: A 1923 painting of the Acropolis from the eighty-fifth volume of *The Studio*, an art magazine that was published in London.

CONTENTS

INTRODUCTION

It is often the case that a major change in government meets heavy resistance from the ruling class if that class doesn't benefit from the change. The ancient Egyptians who immediately preceded the Eighteenth Dynasty fought ferociously to break free from their foreign Hyksos rulers, and later, the transition from republic to empire culminated in Octavian overcoming Mark Anthony and Cleopatra to create the Roman Empire. Even in the case of turning Athens away from aristocratic rule and toward democracy, an event that occurred between the beginning of the Eighteenth Dynasty and the rise of the Roman Empire, there was a massive conflict between Solon and the wealthy old money camp that would lose their influence.

Solon (640 BCE to ca. 561 BCE) was a man who was motivated by his

The Acropolis of Athens with a view of the Parthenon. Pericles had the Parthenon built well after Solon's time.

upbringing to appreciate both aristocratic power and the stifled position of the wealthy merchant. He was born into the aristocracy during the seventh century BCE, but the circumstances of his father's money management made it necessary for him to become a merchant—by default, a position of a lower class. In the spirit of the *Merchant of Venice*, he, as well as the many other people who didn't have immense wealth, depended on sheer luck (as well as the strength of the economy) to not slip any further down in wealth and certainly hoped to avoid the very likely fate of debt slavery. Circumstances would make him the person that the people trusted to deal with this environment of uncertainty and oppression.

As the commander of Greek democracy, Solon would decide what laws to carry over from the old form of government and what laws to add. He would work to relieve the difficult class struggle of many citizens, one that was prolific enough that it threatened to fracture Athenian society. He would also redraw the borders of class so that productivity and wealth, instead of wealth and lineage, would be the characteristics that defined status and influence in the government.

What Solon accomplished serves as a great model for today's democracies. Enabling widespread access to lawful recourse and allowing more people to engage in politics in a way that is beneficial to them is something that every society that cares about democracy aspires to emulate. Representation in a court of law not only created the career of lawyers as advocates, but it also allowed people with poor literacy skills and a weak understanding of law to have a greater chance of success when bringing a lawsuit.

CHAPTER 1

ATHENS: THE ARISTOCRACY

Before Solon, money was the main influencer of Athenian politics. The structure of the Athenian government guaranteed this, but resentment toward the greedy rulers inevitably emerged. Such was the domestic environment of Athens.

RULE BY THE RICH

In ancient times, Greece was wherever Greeks lived. At the time of Solon this included most of what is now Greece, most of southern Italy, the Aegean coast of Turkey, and the western and northern coasts of the Black Sea. All Greeks spoke a common language, although there were several distinct dialects. There was also a common culture, including religious beliefs.

Most Greeks belonged to a polis, or city-state, and each polis had its own unique political arrangements. At any time there might be ten to twenty poleis (the plural of polis) that had influence outside their own territories, but there would be many hundreds of smaller poleis. Some of these smaller poleis cooperated by forming leagues or confederacies with the larger or more powerful poleis.

The Greeks were usually fiercely loyal to their polis, and would see themselves as citizens of Athens, Corinth, or Sparta before they thought of themselves as Greeks. Many would consider exile from their polis as a fate little better than death.

In ancient Greece, each polis was an independent state, even if it only had a few thousand inhabitants. Before the Greeks invented democracy, the aristocracy ran most poleis. Aristocrats were people who owned enough land to be able to exchange the produce from their farms for luxury items, horses, or weapons. Swords were very expensive, so only a few people could own them. The Greeks believed that the only people who should have power in the polis were those who were able to fight to defend it against its enemies.

This 1799 map depicts the individual city-states of ancient Greece. They shared a fairly small space for the number of separate nations that were in Greece.

Because only the wealthy could afford weapons, only the rich had power. Of those who were not aristocrats, most were peasant farmers whose land provided enough food for themselves and their families. The peasants were mostly loyal to the aristocrats because the rich were able to protect the polis from its enemies. There were also a few traders and artisans, who provided services to others.

An important characteristic of the aristocratic families was that they could trace their genealogy back many generations. Often they believed that they were descended from the gods. These families believed that they had always been rich and always owned lots of land.

CORRUPTION

In Athens, the aristocrats, sitting in a council known as the Areopagus, elected magistrates each year. It is thought that the most senior members of each family were members of the Areopagus. The title of the most important magistrate was the archon, who was the head of state. Another was the *polemarch*, who commanded

This depiction of the Areopagus in Athens is based on German painter Julius Schnorr von Carolsfeld's drawing.

the army. There were seven other magistrates: the king archon, who had mostly religious responsibilities, and six decision recorders, who kept a record of all the judgments made by the magistrates, and various other lesser officials. For all except the polemarch, their main job was to act as judges in the law courts.

The aristocrats only elected each other, so the courts would always favor the aristocrats if they had to decide between them and the peasants. What made it even harder for peasants to get justice was that the Athenians did not write down the *nomoi* (singular: *nomos*), the customs or laws. This meant that it was impossible to check whether a judge's decision was right or not. The judge would take into account his own opinion as well as the decisions of other judges in the past. The Athenians did write down the decisions of judges, but since no two cases would ever be exactly the same, a judge did not need to take much notice of them. Having written records would have been of little help to the peasants anyway, since most were probably illiterate. It would be easy for a greedy judge to take someone's land.

Toward the end of the seventh century BCE, trade between Greece and the rest of the Mediterranean world had significantly increased. Many Greek merchants became very rich and were able to buy farms around Athens, the region known as Attica. Such merchants could now afford to pay for weapons and therefore expected a share in power. However, the old money establishment did not allow the merchants to join the aristocracy, which was comprised of a small group of families. The aristocrats did not elect the merchants as magistrates. Even though this newly rich group might have had more wealth than the aristocrats, they were still at a disadvantage when it came to legal and political matters. Their

This illustration from an 1878 book shows ancient Greek merchants moving their goods to a port.

only chance of winning a case in the courts would have been by bribing the magistrate who was acting as a judge. It is easy to see how this situation made the newly rich merchants unhappy. As time went by, more and more merchants gained wealth. The only way they could gain power was to take it by force. In many other Greek poleis during the seventh century, a tyrant who had the support of the merchants seized power.

INVADING ATHENS

Around 632 BCE, Kylon attempted to seize power in Athens in a tyrannical manner. An aristocrat, he was married to the daughter of Theagenes, the tyrant of Megara, a polis neighboring Athens and one of its fiercest enemies.

Kylon had won an event in the Olympic games in 636 BCE. Olympic victors were the celebrities of the ancient Greek world. The Greeks held state dinners in honor of such athletes and gave them the best seats at religious festivals. The ancient Olympic games were different in many ways from the games played today. In ancient times, far fewer events were held, only the winner of an event received recognition, and the games were always held in the same location. Although there were other competitions, the Olympic games were the most prestigious. Competitors came from all over the Greek world to participate.

Kylon attempted to use his prestige as a victorious athlete to start a political career. Kylon came to Athens with a band of armed supporters and friends from Megara, and they seized control of the Acropolis, the hill in the center of the city. Megakles, an aristocrat who was archon that year, brought together the people of Athens and besieged Kylon.

Although the aristocrats were unpopular, Kylon had made a mistake. The ordinary people of Athens were not yet so unhappy that they would allow someone who had joined forces with their enemy to control their polis.

Kylon managed to escape secretly, but his supporters were not so lucky. Their food ran out, and they took sanctuary in one of the temples. Megakles broke the deadlock by persuading them to come out in exchange for the promise of

This Alberto Salinas painting from the twentieth century shows Greeks competing in the race of the four-horse chariot.

a fair trial. As they were coming out of the temple, Megakles and his supporters attacked and murdered them. Megakles died soon afterward, but the Athenians never forgot this crime.

Historians presume that Kylon never returned to Athens, but his family was still there. There was increasing tension between the families of Megakles and Kylon, and eventually the children of Megakles were put on trial for sacrilege and sent into exile. However, they returned a few years later when the archon was more friendly to them. For the next two hundred years, the descendants of Megakles were exiled whenever their political enemies were in power, and they were recalled when their friends were in control.

THE OLYMPIC GAMES

Many myths surround the conception of the ancient Olympic games. The name "Olympic" is an adjective that invokes Mount Olympus, the mythical home of the Greek gods, and calls into consideration a myth in which the guardians of Zeus, during his infancy, completed a footrace. In other tellings Zeus himself may have begun the games to celebrate his dominance over Cronus.

Whether or not they had divine beginnings, many of the first games consisted only of a footrace. That event was extended, and more events were added. Eventually, the Olympic games would include a pentathlon and wrestling. Those who traveled to the site of the games were protected under an order of peace regardless of the tension between the Greek city-states, and the winners of the games (there was no prize for second place) would enjoy a popularity akin to the immortality of the gods, with perks like having their statue placed in Olympia and their meals paid for by the public.

The Roman Empire would ban the Olympic games at around 394 CE because of its significance in pagan tradition.

IGNORING THE CONSTITUTION

Up to the seventh century BCE, all poleis were run by aristocrats who ruled for their own benefit. Normally there was a balance of power, and the different families would take turns holding the magistracies. However, an aristocrat who became more powerful than the others because of popular support might take control and rule as an individual with supreme power. Such an individual ruler was called a tyrant. Usually the tyrant became powerful enough to take control because of support from the newly rich merchant class.

The merchant class in a polis had no political rights, and they would support anyone who promised to make their lives better. If a tyrant was ruling the polis, no one else had real political power. Although the tyrant might keep the old system of magistrates, he would ensure that only his friends and supporters were chosen. The lives of the merchants were better because under a tyrant they received equal treatment with the aristocrats. Because they had supported the tyrant, he would tend to favor their interests. For example, a tyrant

The court of Areopagus could only be influenced by the aristocratic class because the political structure of Greece favored them over everyone else.

might try to make trading easier for those he favored.

Another feature of Greek tyrants was that they supported each other. It was very common for one tyrant to be connected to another by marriage. A tyrant, for instance, might be married to the daughter of another. Sometimes, if a tyrant was threatened with revolution, other tyrants would send soldiers to help prevent it. Although each polis was independent, when tyrants were in charge there were networks of alliances between them.

At some time or other in the history of almost every polis, a tyrant ruled it. Some poleis were ruled by a series of tyrants over hundreds of years, with sons inheriting power from their fathers. In others, after a while the people threw out the tyrant and set up a democracy. This was possible because the tyrants had already taken power away from the aristocrats.

Tyrants came to power with popular support. When a tyrant died, if his son was not popular the son would have to use force to keep control. It was often the sons or grandsons of the original tyrants who were thrown out in a revolution. The less popular the new tyrant was, the more brutal the regime had to be, and this increased the chances of a revolution.

Today, the word "tyrant" means a brutal dictator. But for the Greeks, a tyrant's status was defined by the method of gaining power. Seizing power through unconstitutional or hereditary means made a tyrant.

DRACONIAN NEW LAWS

Kylon had come close to overthrowing the aristocracy, and the rivalry between the families of Kylon and Megakles threatened to break out into violence at any time. This situation greatly worried the aristocrats. They did not wish to give anyone else a chance to exploit the unhappiness of the newly rich merchant class. And so, in 621 BCE, the aristocrats who ruled Athens decided to ask a man called Draco to produce some nomoi, or laws, to keep peace and order.

We know nothing about what Draco's nomoi were. Solon repealed all of the nomoi of Draco, except for one about homicide, and the Athenians quickly forgot them. Legend tells us that they were very harsh. The English word "draconian," meaning "very harsh," comes from his name. Athenians later said that Draco gave the death penalty for most crimes, even stealing fruit. The story goes that when someone asked Draco why this was, he answered that he thought that minor crimes deserved death, and he could think of no worse punishment for serious ones.

Whatever they were really like, the nomoi of Draco certainly did not keep the peace. The merchant class continued to be unhappy at their lack of political power, and as their numbers increased, they must have seemed more threatening than ever. Their rivalry with the aristocrats showed no signs of abating. To make matters worse, by the end of

This eighteenth-century engraving depicts Draco, the particularly harsh lawgiver whose reforms did not appease the merchant class.

the seventh century BCE a new problem appeared. This was the problem of debt.

FARMING DIFFICULTIES

Although the precise reasons are not clear today, many peasant farmers in Solon's time got themselves into debt. Traditionally, farmers must live on credit until they can sell their harvests. Perhaps the harvest was bad several years in a row. Or, possibly, the aristocrats who ran the courts became greedy when they saw the increased wealth of the merchants and began to make life more difficult for the peasants through taxation. Or, it could be that the big farms of the aristocrats produced extra grain, and its price fell. This would mean that farmers would need more land to produce the same value of grain as in the past, and they could only get more land and the tools to work it by borrowing from the aristocrats.

The problem for the peasants was that if they were unable to repay their loans by the deadline, their creditors could force them and their families into slavery. As slaves, they were subject to the whims of their owners, who could either keep them or sell them to someone else. Sometimes the

Many in ancient Greece lived under a lot of pressure. These farmers could lose everything with a single bad harvest.

purchasers of these newly enslaved people were foreigners, and they transported their new slaves to another part of Greece or the Mediterranean. It seems that many peasants who were about to become slaves because of debt left Athens and went to live abroad voluntarily. It was better for them to be free than enslaved, wherever they had to live.

Many poor Athenian farmers became *hektemoroi*. This was a form of tenant farming. The name means "sixth-parters." Scholars are uncertain whether this indicated that the farmers paid one-sixth of their produce to a landowner as rent or they kept one-sixth of their produce as pay. If they paid one-sixth, then the five-sixths they kept seemed to be plenty, and their lives would not have been very difficult. If the farmers only kept one-sixth, that amount seems much too little to live on. Modern historians cannot agree on this. Perhaps if peasants paid one-sixth, it was not one-sixth of their produce, but one-sixth of the value of their land, though we have no idea how that could be assessed. Or if they kept one-sixth, perhaps they only kept one-sixth of the grain, but were able to keep all the other produce of their farms. Either of these situations would mean that life was hard but livable. What we are certain of is that the hektemoroi were unhappy about their status. They likely became hektemoroi because of some kind of debt. Once they were in this position, there was no way out. It was impossible for them to improve their status. The hektemoroi were regarded as little better than slaves. And, if they did not work hard enough for the landowner, it is possible that they actually became slaves.

CHAPTER 2

THE RISE OF SOLON

Athens' relation to the rest of the world was one factor that contributed to the popularity of Solon. His positive interactions in trade built his wealth and defined his social status, while his leadership and involvement in various conflicts led those around him to trust his judgement. With another election coming up, and his popularity soaring higher than ever before, the Athenians would act on how they felt toward his ideology.

SLAVERY

Various forms of slavery existed in the ancient world. The most common was chattel slavery.

A chattel slave was the property of an individual ("chattel" is an old word for property).

Chattel slaves could be acquired in various ways. After military victories, for example, captives were often sold as slaves. Pirates might take prisoners from coastal settlements and enslave them. The slave trade thrived throughout the Mediterranean, with slave traders shipping their cargo from one region to another, so slaves were usually not indigenous to the land in which they were forced to work.

This wash drawing shows prisoners of war, a group of foreigners likely to fall into slavery, being sold in ancient Greece.

Any children of slaves were slaves themselves, so slaves could be obtained by deliberate breeding as well. If an owner had a number of chattel slaves, both male and female, it was not unusual for the slaves to form relationships and have children. However, the owner could sell one or both parents, or any of the children, and split up the family, especially since the slave had no legal rights.

The type of work done could range from household duties or running the owner's shop to working on a farm or in a mine.

Another type of slavery occurred when one polis conquered another. The victors forced the entire defeated population to work for them, without moving them from their farms. These slaves were owned by the polis and could only be sold by the polis, not by individuals. This type of slavery did not exist in Athens.

In addition, the word "slave" could indicate anyone who was forced to work for someone else due to legal obligations. This kind of slave could not be sold. In contrast, a hired laborer had to work to get food, but was not forced to do so, and could choose to starve instead. This use of the word "slave" indicates someone who did not have free choices in everything, but who was not a slave in the strictest sense.

In the time of Solon, only the wealthy could afford to own slaves, and most productive work was still performed by those who were free. It was only later that Athens became wealthy enough for slave ownership to be common. Slavery was an accepted part of life, but probably did not make much difference in most people's lives—at least, that is, until they found themselves in debt and risked becoming enslaved.

MONEY EMERGES

The whole economy of the Mediterranean world was also beginning to change at this time. In what is now modern Turkey, coins were invented around 630 BCE. Today, it is hard to imagine a world without money, but back then it was a new invention, and it took time for people to get used to the idea. Farmers had always exchanged part of their crops for other goods that they could not grow or make for themselves. If they needed iron to make a plough, they could swap grain for it. They could easily see how the labor they put into their crops could be converted into goods. As such, it took some time

The gold coins of Croesus and the silver Macedonian tetradrachm were likely the first coins to be used as money.

for people to accept that a coin, a small disc of silver, could be accepted as payment and later traded for a certain amount of goods, such as olive oil.

THE PROS AND CONS OF MONEY

While money is the common form of payment today, in ancient times, people used a barter system, in which an item's worth was determined by comparison to another item. But bartering one set of items—olives, for example—with different groups who have another set of items—perhaps barley—could result in different prices, depending on which group the merchant approaches with his olives. Or, the quality of ingredients may vary from one trade to the next, even when trading with the same group. Another important element of a barter system is that the two groups who are trading actually want what the other group has—otherwise, they wouldn't trade at all. And, some goods could rot, thus destroying the wealth that they once held.

In comparison, money offered people a single standard of value. But, money's value frequently fluctuated and was tied to the material that the money was made from. Money with no value had no practical purpose, although goods in fine shape were always useful in themselves. Forged money, or money that could easily be forged, could cause people to lose faith in the value of money, or it could cause the theft of goods through deceit. Money would last much longer than goods, but could easily be stolen. There is also the matter that money, as a new concept, could potentially require a major leap of faith for people who had never used it.

Since the aristocrats controlled the production of coins, they were able to decide how much the coins were worth. For the first time it was possible to have banks. It was easier to store wealth because coins did not rot and perish like grain could. Aristocrats had always exchanged precious metals for luxury items, so the change was not so great for them. But it was a new experience for the peasant farmers to deal with objects that had no practical use to them.

The Athenians did not produce their own coins until around 575 BCE, and we do not know how much impact foreign currency had on the Athenian economy before Solon's reforms in 594 BCE. But this new invention would change the world forever. The aristocrats were in a position to take advantage of the peasants as they could demand payment for debts in currency, which was always scarce with poor farmers. The aristocrats could then enslave the peasants when payments could not be made. The new style of doing business could only have made the situation worse.

One way or another, the people of Athens were unhappy. The aristocrats feared someone might try to become a tyrant. Kylon had come close, and the new laws of Draco had not helped. Everyone else had good reason to want change. The merchants were angry because they had no share of political power. Peasant farmers were suffering from debt and the danger of being made into slaves. The hektemoroi were unhappy because of their hard lives and lack of freedom. If the situation continued, the polis might descend into chaos. So in 594 BCE the

After Solon issued the laws he saw fit for Athens to follow, it was important that everyone read them.

Athenians turned to Solon. The aristocrats elected him archon, giving him complete power to change everything as long as he would prevent the crisis they feared.

SHAPING SOLON

The details of Solon's early life are sketchy. His father was Exekestides and his mother was related to Peisistratos. Her name is unknown today. Historians estimate that Solon was born around 640 BCE and died in 561 BCE or a little later, at the age of eighty.

Solon's family was in the aristocracy, but they weren't one of the richest. The education of aristocratic boys consisted of learning to read and write, as well as some kind of musical training, most likely singing and playing the lyre. Solon would have studied Homer, perhaps even memorizing his poems. The verse of Homer, according to aristocratic Greeks in Solon's time, contained everything that a respectable Greek needed to know about religion and proper behavior. Boys would have participated in some physical education as well. Athletics and wrestling were considered suitable

This colored engraving by Heinrich Leutemann shows merchants, who often relied on trade by sea to import and export their goods.

for aristocratic young men. In his late teens and early twenties, Solon may well have received some basic military training, too.

The legends about Solon say that his father, Exekestides, was very generous to the needy, so generous in fact that there was very little left for Solon to inherit when his father died. As a result, Solon

became a merchant, sailing around the Mediterranean to make a living. In that era, such activities were not undertaken by a respectable aristocrat. For the Greeks, the only respectable source of income for an aristocrat was from the land. However, Solon's choices were limited, so he set off to make his fortune.

The situation proved advantageous for Solon. During his travels, he saw the different ways that other poleis and non-Greek states organized their constitutions. This experience would have helped him a great deal when he came to change the Athenian constitution.

RALLYING THE ATHENIANS

One episode that shows the profile Solon had in Athenian public life before he was elected archon was the capture of the island of Salamis, which lies just off the coast of Attica, the territory of Athens. Its strategic location controlled access to the harbors of Athens. The Athenians seem to have fought a long war against Megara for control of Salamis. Megara was just along the coast of Athens, and Salamis was very close to the harbor of Megara. It is not known who originally owned the island, but certainly the Athenians believed that it ought to be theirs.

Sometime just after 600 BCE, the Megarians managed to take control of Salamis so decisively that the Athenians decided to give up the fight. The Athenians went so far as to pass a law stating that anyone who proposed restarting the war for Salamis should be put to death. It seems that Solon was unwilling to settle for this. So he had his family tell people that he had gone mad. Then one day he rushed into the marketplace. A big crowd gathered to find out what this man, whom they believed to be mad, would do. Solon recited a poem he had composed, which began, "As my own herald I have come from lovely Salamis,/ Having composed ordered words, a song instead of a speech." And he went on to urge the Athenians, "Let us go to Salamis, fight for that lovely island/ And fling off our bitter disgrace." The Athenians were so moved by Solon's poem that they changed the law again and decided to make another attempt to capture Salamis. The story seems fanciful, but there is no reason to doubt the authenticity of the poem. The story may be essentially true as well.

Under the leadership of Solon, the Athenians managed to recapture Salamis. Exactly how this was done is unknown because the stories are rather confused. However, one version claims that Solon called for five hundred volunteers and promised them that they would govern the island if they captured it. If this is what happened, then it reveals how bad conditions were for most Athenians. The prospect of having political rights in Athens itself must have seemed so low that these volunteers were willing to risk their lives and then to move themselves and their families across the water to an island that would possibly be a battlefield again. Perhaps it was the strength of desire for political rights that gave these volunteers the morale to win the battle for Salamis. Although there was more fighting to come, Salamis did end up as part of Athenian territory. Years later, a statue of Solon was in the main town on the island, and the people of Salamis could point out a temple to Ares, the god of

This 1828 painting by Merry-Joseph Blondel depicts Solon contemplating either poetry or laws.

war, which they believed Solon had built. There was even a legend that after Solon's death, his ashes were sprinkled over the island. The advice Solon gave in this event was one crucial factor in the Athenians' decision to appoint him archon.

KRISA

After the victory at Salamis, it seems that Solon may have been chosen as an ambassador for Athens. Following that, he gave advice to the Greeks to ensure the independence of the oracle at Delphi. An oracle, according to the Greeks, was someone who could receive messages directly from the gods. The temple of the Delphic Oracle was the most sacred site in Greece, and the Amphiktyonic League had been established to protect it. The Amphiktyonic League was a group of poleis, including Athens, that had sworn to cooperate to protect the sacredness of Delphi. They would send ambassadors to twice yearly meetings.

At one of these meetings, league members discussed what to do about the polis of Krisa, which was making life difficult for people visiting the Oracle. Krisa controlled the road to Delphi and was forcing people to pay tolls. At the meeting of the

This is an old road to Delphi that Krisa may have controlled to keep visitors from seeing the oracle.

league, Solon advised the Greeks that they could not allow themselves to be prevented from using the oracle freely and that they should go to war to guarantee its freedom. They took his advice, and Krisa was destroyed in what was called a "sacred war."

A NEW ARCHON

Solon had come to the attention of the Athenians in very dramatic ways, and his advice had worked to their advantage. As such, it was logical that the aristocrats looked to him when they finally decided to do something about the political crisis facing Athens.

Solon must have seemed a good choice for more general reasons as well. He was an aristocrat, but he was not from an extremely rich family. This meant two things. First, there would be no reason for other aristocrats to be jealous of his position. The most influential families were the richest, and no doubt the richest few families would be in constant competition to get their own members into the magistracies. Solon came from outside this circle of competing families, and therefore he would not upset the balance too much. Second and just as important was that Solon was politically prominent by virtue of the good advice he had been giving and not simply by his aristocratic background. As a result, the poorer sections of Athenian society could trust him to be fair to them. In addition, the fact that Solon had spent time as a merchant must have made him an acceptable mediator to the newly rich, who had made most of their money through trade.

And, of course, there were Solon's poems. It seems that Solon gave recitals of his poetry, in which he commented on the state of affairs in Athens. No doubt Solon produced poetry partly because he enjoyed it, but also because he lived in a society that valued the spoken word. Although most Athenians could probably read a little, few would have been able to write well. Thus, almost all communication had to be spoken. In addition, poetry is easier to remember than prose, so it is natural to use this method if the purpose is to give people something to go away with and discuss. The Greek world had a long tradition of using poetry to give advice. The Greeks would look in the works of Homer, the earliest Greek poet, for advice on subjects like religion and fighting wars. Another of the earliest Greek poets, Hesiod, wrote about religion and farming.

It is unknown whether Solon wrote his poems because he hoped to get the position of archon, or whether he simply wanted to advise the Athenians about social issues. His concern for Athens seems genuine. One of his poems began, "I am aware, and pain lies heavy in my heart,/ That I watch the oldest Ionian state [Athens] sinking." There can be no doubt that Solon knew about the troubles facing Athens. And he seems to have blamed the wealthy in his poems, "They are rich because they trust in unjust methods." At the time Solon was elected, one of his phrases was going around Athens: "Equality creates no conflict." Apparently, the rich thought that he meant equality of opportunity, and the poor thought he meant equality of land ownership—sharing the land equally.

At an official meeting of the Areopagus, many men, all aristocrats, listen as one man makes his case or proposes a referendum.

Solon was elected archon in 594 BCE, with full powers to reform the constitution as he thought best. The election was probably by a show of hands at a meeting of the Areopagus, the council of aristocrats. All sides thought that Solon would benefit them. The changes he made earned him the reputation, two hundred years later, of being the father of democracy.

CHAPTER 3

RESTRUCTURING ATHENS

Many of Solon's actions changed the face of Athens. Class struggle was something he cared about greatly, so the reforms he offered gave opportunities to those who were once in a very different position. He was aware that reforming government structures would allow these changes to last, so he also took that into consideration.

DEALING WITH DEBT

One of the main problems facing Athens was debt. Solon's first order of action was to decree a broad cancellation of debts. The details of this action are sketchy today, but it came to be known by the name *seisachtheia*, which means the "shaking off of burdens." It is unlikely that Solon actually used the word himself, since it is in none of his surviving

This illustration depicts Solon dictating his laws to the Athenian record keepers.

poetry, so the word was probably first used by later writers.

One of the stories told about Solon is that just before he passed his law canceling debts, he mentioned his plans to some aristocratic friends. They took the opportunity to borrow large amounts of money, knowing that they would not have to repay it. However, when people realized what had happened,

Solon's friends were disgraced. This nearly ruined Solon's political career because he had leaked the information. But Solon was able to demonstrate that he had personally lost what he had lent out previously. It is likely that the allegations were false and were just devised by someone who was unhappy with Solon's cancellation of debt or his other reforms.

The story does reveal that the cancellation likely applied to all debts, and not just those of a selected few or to a certain amount of someone's overall debt. However, canceling all debt was an extremely radical thing to do, so there remains some doubt as to whether that is actually what Solon did.

SLAVERY AND DEBT

Another important problem that deeply concerned the poorest farmers was the threat of falling into slavery. Solon set free anyone who had been enslaved because of debt. He also brought home those who had been sold to foreigners, or who had gone into exile because of debt. His poetry provides evidence of this:

> I brought back to their divinely-founded
> home many Athenians

> Who had been sold abroad, either illegally
>
> Or legally, and those whom poverty had driven away,
>
> And no longer spoke the Attic dialect because of their exile.
>
> And I set free those who had been made slaves
>
> Here at home, and feared their masters.

Again, the fact that slaves were released was effectively a complete cancellation of the debt for which they had been enslaved. The return of those who had gone into exile because they were unable to pay their debts also required the cancellation of those debts. Some aristocrats who sold people into slavery because of their debts had not always followed the nomoi, or law. They must have seized the land of peasants and sold the farmers into slavery without going through the proper process.

No form of compensation for the debts that were cancelled could have been made because at that time Athens would not have had reserves of wealth to use for this purpose. Taxes were collected, but only on a small scale, and only enough to pay for what was needed. No government treasury existed that might be tapped for compensation to the slaveholders. This created a problem in bringing home any Athenians who had been sold to foreign owners. Their new owners were not Athenians, so no law passed by Solon could force them to give up their slaves. Someone would have to buy back the slaves. This could only be done by the Athenian aristocrats who sold them initially. The profits from the sale of slaves now had to be used to buy back the slaves.

REMOVING THE HOROI

Another aspect of the seisachtheia was the removal of *horoi* (stones used to mark the boundaries of land ownership). Solon wrote, "From the black Earth I/ Pulled up the horoi that had been planted everywhere,/ So what was formerly enslaved is now free." Considerable debate exists among historians regarding what the removal of the horoi would achieve. The normal meaning of horoi is "boundary markers." It was considered a very serious religious offence to remove such markers, and simply removing boundaries would not do anything to help the peasant farmers. The other meaning of *horos* is "mortgage stone," indicating that a horos was placed upon land which was bought with the help of a loan. If the loan was not repaid, then the lender could take the farmer into slavery and also take possession of the land. When Solon cancelled the debts, it would be natural to remove the stone giving evidence of the loan. Solon effectively made the land obtained through a loan fully the property of the borrower. This would explain what Solon meant in his poem. However, the first evidence for the use of the word "horos" as meaning "mortgage stone" is not until 364 BCE, more than two hundred years after Solon was archon. In addition, archaeologists have not uncovered any stone inscribed with mortgage agreements from before this later date.

It remains unclear what Solon was doing when he pulled up the horoi. However, one other

A horos stone in Athens, Greece. This one served as a boundary marker.

possibility exists. Perhaps the removal of the horoi is related to the return of those who had gone abroad as slaves or exiles. If an aristocrat had taken the land, he would have extended his own boundary markers to show this fact. When the former owners returned to their land, they would have wanted only their own markers on it. If it was considered wrong for the original owner to lose the land because of debt, then there would be no problem in pulling up the wrongfully planted horoi. Just as the original owner had been unjustly enslaved, the land had been made a slave to someone who was not its rightful owner.

ABOLISHING THE HEKTEMOROI

As a further part of the seisachtheia, Solon abolished the class of hektemoroi (tenant farmers). As noted earlier, historians are unsure about the specifics of the hektemoroi. By the time the Athenians wrote about them, the hektemoroi were long gone, and no one could remember exactly what their position had been. If, as seems likely, they had become hektemoroi because of debt,

WEALTH REDISTRIBUTION

Wealth redistribution is a trademark of socialism. But for redistribution to happen, the group that holds the most power must be sympathetic to the needs of the lower classes.

This kind of redistribution has many forms. A society whose government depends on taxes can receive disproportionate tax payments so that the burden is heavier on the wealthy. But there must also be a giving element or the money simply benefits the government without improving the situation of the poor. Education, food distribution, health care, and other programs can help people who are unable to afford such resources. Land seizures, to be redistributed by a universal lottery or given to those who occupied the land, could also redistribute wealth. And in societies that have such institutions as slavery and prisons, the work and freedom of unpaid workers, however they came to losing the benefits of freedom, can be restored to those individuals.

the cancellation of debt would have removed their obligations to the landowners. Quite possibly Solon also gave them the land on which they worked (it may well have belonged to them originally in any case). In addition to changing the status of those who were hektemoroi in 594 BCE, Solon also changed the system so that people could no longer become hektemoroi in the future.

Clearly, the seisachtheia had a major impact on the lives of most Athenians. Those who were poor had a chance at a fresh start in life. Those who were wealthy lost out. No doubt some of them lost huge amounts, both in terms of land and slaves. The gap between rich and poor had been reduced, at least for a time, and Solon must have felt that this would help to stop the crisis that was threatening the stability of the state.

NEW CLASSES

While the seisachtheia helped to make life better for the peasant farmers, it would not have made much difference to the merchant class. What they wanted was a share of power. Before Solon's reign the aristocrats had kept the magistracies for themselves. In order for Solon to open up the magistracies to non-aristocrats, he had to change the qualifications for election.

This nineteenth-century wood engraving depicts day laborers of ancient Athens. Their wealth is not indicated clearly in this illustration.

Previously, aristocratic birth had been required. This was why the merchant class could not get into office no matter how rich they became. They simply could not change the fact that they were not of noble birth. So Solon divided the people of Athens into four classes based on property:

the *pentakosiomedimnoi* ("five-hundred bushellers"), the *hippeis* ("horsemen"), the *zeugitae* ("yokemen"), and the *thetes* ("day laborers"). It is likely that the last three classes already existed in some form and that Solon simply organized them more effectively. These three groups relate to military service, since the hippeis could afford horses to ride into battle, the zeugitae could pay for armor to fight on foot, and the thetes were too poor to buy any armor. Solon probably created the pentakosiomedimnoi as a new class, as the name is so specific that it does not seem to be a natural one. It is possible that the word already existed and meant something quite general, like the word "millionaire."

All of this only applied to the free Athenians. Slaves had no rights and were not even regarded as Athenians. In any case, many of them were of foreign origin.

GOVERNMENTAL CHANGES

The impact of what Solon did was to specify exactly what official positions and rights each group should have. This was what allowed the newly rich to break through into positions of power. Solon enacted a law stating that the pentakosiomedimnoi were eligible for the position of archon and other official posts. The lesser magistracies were opened to the hippeis. Most important, Solon made membership of each class dependent on wealth, not birth. If the merchants were wealthy enough to be pentakosiomedimnoi, they could also be elected archon, or one of the magistrates, giving them a share of power. However, the fact that the newly rich were eligible for election did not guarantee that they would be elected, because the electors were still the members of the Areopagus, the council of aristocrats.

No doubt a few of the merchants were popular enough (or hosted good enough parties) that they were elected. Also, it is possible that aristocratic families had to marry their sons to the daughters of the merchant class to bring extra wealth into their families, which would have created political alliances. To ensure that the rest of the newly rich merchants were not excluded from power, Solon changed the Areopagus so that its members were those who had held one of the nine official positions just below the archon. These officials became life members of the Areopagus. As the newly rich were occasionally elected, their influence gradually increased because after their year in office they became electors themselves.

Some doubt exists regarding exactly how the different property classes were organized. The name of the pentakosiomedimnoi means those with five hundred *medimnoi*. A *medimnos* was a Greek measure of capacity, roughly equal to eight gallons (thirty liters), or a bushel, hence the name is often translated as "five hundred bushellers." This class, at least, is clear enough. Solon picked out those whose farms produced a large quantity of grain each year as being rich enough to be suitable to help govern the polis. Five hundred medimnoi equate to about fifteen tons of barley, which is enough to feed more than seventy-five people for a year. This figure, however, does not provide a full picture of the productivity of such farms. For example, additional produce was not measured by the medimnos—wine, olive oil, and livestock—and did not therefore count toward the assessment. In this era, no machines were available to help do the work, and so this level of production implies very large farms and a great deal of wealth.

ASSESSING PRODUCTIVITY

In ancient times it was believed that Solon also set levels of production for the other classes: three hundred medimnoi for the hippeis, and two hundred bushels for the zeugitae. All those whose land

A bronze spearhead like this one was almost certainly used by the ancient Athenian infantry.

produced less than two hundred medimnoi of grain or who had no land at all were classified as thetes. It seems likely that later writers invented these levels of production and that Solon never actually applied them. Such levels imply a degree of wealth that was very high. If these quotas existed, many of those in the previous class of zeugitae would not have qualified to stay in their class and would have become thetes. As such, they would have had fewer rights under Solon than they previously had, which seems unlikely.

It is also difficult to know how each farmer would be assessed, since there was no census or bureau of taxation with the kind of records required. It is most likely that the hippeis and zeugitae were still assessed in terms of their ability to provide the weapons and equipment of cavalry and infantry respectively. Their equipment provided visible evidence of which class they belonged to, so no one would be in any doubt. Similarly, it must have been clear who produced enough from their farms to be counted as pentakosiomedimnoi simply by observing their lifestyle. If a dispute arose at any time, then it would be possible for the appropriate magistrate to make a more formal assessment, but this must have been the exception rather than the rule. Certainly a regular assessment of all Athenians would have been out of the question.

The thetes had only basic rights, and they were those Athenians who worked as hired laborers, or perhaps had a small market stall. They probably had to work very hard for a living and must have had very little time to spare for thinking about political rights.

FROM CUSTOMS TO LAWS

Solon had removed the immediate threat of a crisis with the seisachtheia and his reform of the constitution to allow the newly rich merchant class access to power. But he also realized that Athenian society needed further reform to avoid problems that might arise in the future. What Athens needed was *eunomia*, the principle of "good order" through the law. As he said in a poem, " Laws which are equal for peasant and noble/ Providing fair justice to each I wrote."

The Athenians remembered Solon most of all for his role as a lawgiver. More important, for the first time in Athenian history, Solon had all the nomoi

The Greeks of ancient Athens owed their new understanding of the law to Solon's efforts to make it accessible.

written down. The nomoi changed from customs to laws. Instead of magistrates deciding legal cases on the basis of their own opinions and what had customarily been done in the past, Solon's reforms required officials to follow the law as it existed in written form for all citizens to see. This change from unwritten to written laws was vital for personal freedom. For the first time it was possible to check if what a magistrate decided was fair. Not only could justice be done, justice was seen to be done.

Solon must have recorded all the nomoi that he knew and also spoke to other magistrates to find out what they thought the nomoi were in the past. Then he would have compared what he had put together with all the decisions that magistrates had recorded in previous years. Some of the nomoi would have been applied consistently, but others must have been used very inconsistently. Solon had to decide the fairest way to record each nomos so that it became an unchangeable law. Most likely, the nomoi of Draco were probably not written down or only a select few were.

Not only did Solon record the nomoi as laws, he had them posted in the marketplace where people could see them. Everyone had the chance to find out exactly what the law said before appearing in a court. Everyone could tell if the magistrate was applying the law correctly. Instead of being controlled and kept secret by aristocrats, the law became public property.

However, it was no use knowing that a magistrate was not applying the law correctly if nothing could be done about it. So Solon introduced the right of appeal. This was the best way to protect the peasants from the aristocrats. To make the protection even better, Solon ordered that appeals be heard by a court of adult male Athenians. This popular court was called the Heliaia. Every adult male Athenian was allowed to take part in hearings, and decisions were made by a vote. This meant that even the lowest class, the thetes, could take part in running Athens. If the peasants felt threatened by the decision of a magistrate, they could turn out in force and defeat it.

SIMPLIFYING THE LEGAL SYSTEM

Together, the written laws and the right of appeal made the whole Athenian legal system much fairer.

It was not perfect, however. Not all Athenians would have been well enough educated or literate enough to interpret the laws properly. And not all Athenians would have had the confidence to stand up in front of a magistrate, or even the Heliaia (which could be thousands strong) and argue their cases. Solon could do little about illiteracy, since there was no state education system in Athens and no resources to provide one even if he had wanted to do this. But Solon tackled the problem of citizens feeling intimidated as he changed the law so that anyone could bring a charge against someone who was accused of a crime. Previously only the person who was the victim of the crime, or close family members, could bring charges, and it was the person who brought the charges who had to stand up in court. By allowing anyone to bring charges, Solon took the first step toward the creation of professional lawyers who could fight a case on someone else's behalf.

In practice, this change may have helped aristocrats to bring political charges against their enemies, by pretending to support some needy person or other. It probably would have been a very serious crime for peasants to persuade someone else to take the time and trouble to fight cases for them. However, the principle was established, and it made justice a little more accessible for those in the lower class.

SOLON'S LAWS

It is unknown today how many of the laws that later Athenians believed originated with Solon were actually his, but many probably were. One in particular, the law forbidding loans secured by a person's freedom, was definitely his. This meant that it was no longer possible for someone who could not repay a loan to be enslaved. This protected the peasants from sinking back into the kind of financial problems and debt that had made the seisachtheia necessary. Conversely, it meant that the very poor might have nothing at all to offer as a guarantee that they would repay loans, making it impossible for them to borrow money to improve their situations in life.

One other law, usually credited to Solon, allowed property to be willed to someone who was not a blood relative. If someone had no sons to inherit his property (and only men could own property at that time), he was allowed in his will to adopt someone from outside the family as a son. This newly created heir would then inherit and continue the family line.

Many laws attributed to Solon were probably not his creations. A man caught in adultery could be killed without fear of punishment, and a woman caught in adultery was forbidden to wear jewelry and could have any punishment other than mutilation or death inflicted upon her. Drunkenness in a magistrate was punishable by death. At night a thief could be killed instantly; in the day he had to be taken before the court. It was forbidden to speak ill of the dead. All these are genuine Athenian laws, but it is unlikely that Solon created them. Either they were older nomoi that Solon wrote down, or they were added to the list later. One of the problems historians face is that after the nomoi were recorded and displayed in public, new laws were simply added at the end of Solon's list. It was quickly forgotten that they were not there originally, and so after a few years any law on the public list was thought to be part of the laws of Solon.

ECONOMIC REFORMS

The Athenians believed that Solon carried out a number of economic reforms, and it is possible that this was the case. Some laws relating to farming were attributed to Solon, such as the rule that trees had to be planted at least 5 feet (1.5 meters) from a neighbor's land, or that bee hives had to be at least 300 feet (91 m) from a neighbor's hives. But historians do not specifically know the origin of many of these laws.

However, historians today do believe that Solon was genuinely responsible for certain reforms, including a temporary prohibition on the export of farm produce apart from olive oil and a law granting citizenship to skilled foreign craftsmen who immigrated to Athens. The latter measure encouraged the development of small-scale industries and trade in finished products. The former measure would have prevented aristocrats from using their surplus grain to obtain luxuries, and it would have kept more grain in Attica, thus keeping the price down so that the peasants could afford it. The only product that Attica had too much of was olive oil, so this was excluded from the ban.

Grain (usually barley), olives, and grapes were the staple crops. Most Athenians would have lived on a diet of barley, olives, fish, wine, and cheese (from goat's milk). Few could afford to eat meat except on special occasions. Olive oil could be used for many purposes, from cooking oil to fuel for lamps.

Soon after the time of Solon, Athens began to surpass the polis of Corinth as the place where the best Greek pottery was produced. This may have been a coincidence, but it does suggest that Solon had made life easier for foreign craftsmen. However, no evidence exists to support the idea that a shortage of grain occurred in Attica at the time of Solon. But there clearly was such a shortage in the fifth century, so the export ban may well not be genuine. Most Greek poleis were normally more or less self-sufficient in their food requirements.

Solon also changed the Athenian system of weights and measures. Up until Solon's time, Athens had used the Aeginetan system, but Solon changed to the Euboic standard. In the Aeginetan standard, a drachma (the basic unit of currency) equaled about six and one-third grams of silver. Under the Euboic standard, the drachma equaled four and one-quarter grams of silver. Because

This painting shows some of the early stages of olive oil production: harvesting and pressing the olives.

most of the principal trading poleis of Greece used the Euboic standard, this change allowed Athens to trade and compete with them more easily, strengthening the Athenian economy. The ancient writers believed that Solon changed the coinage at the same time or even issued the first Athenian coins. Modern archaeology shows that this cannot have been the case. As noted previously, the earliest Athenian coins date to about 575 BCE, some twenty years after Solon was archon. Nevertheless, with these other economic reforms, Athens would have been in a better position to take advantage of coins when they were introduced.

CHAPTER 4

THE CRISIS AND THE CURE

The people chose Solon to deal with the likelihood of revolt. He offered many reforms, but after that, he disappeared for a great deal of time. While his absence had some particularly harmful consequences, his reforms ultimately offered a massive change in the mentality of the Athenians when it came to the relationship between governing and wealth.

MAKING EUNOMIA

Solon believed that with the seisachtheia, the new system of classes, and the written laws he had put forth Athens had a chance at eunomia (good order). He claimed that:

> To the people I have given as much as they deserve,

> Neither taking away their rights nor giving too much.
>
> Those who had power and were admired for their wealth,
>
> I have made sure they suffered no indignity.
>
> I have stood with a strong shield flung around both sides,
>
> And not allowed either an unfair victory.

But some Athenians, those whose privileges were now restricted, thought that Solon's reforms had cost them too much, and they complained bitterly. A fragment of one of Solon's poems reads, "In great works to please everyone is difficult." Elsewhere Solon wrote: "Everyone thought they would make a fortune/...and now they are angry with me,/ And all give me sideways glances as if I were an enemy."

According to the legends, Solon left Athens for ten years, having made a law that no one could change any of what he had done without his agreement. It is not known what Solon did on these travels. Perhaps he went back to being a merchant, or maybe he simply enjoyed traveling. Most important, he wanted to avoid Athenians asking him questions about his reforms. They had to take responsibility for making the reforms work.

Solon traveled around the Mediterranean, probably visiting Egypt and Cyprus, before

This 1629 painting shows King Croesus of Lydia receiving tribute from one of his subjects.

returning to Athens. One famous story tells how he visited the court of Croesus, king of Lydia, an area of modern Turkey. Croesus was famous for his wealth. He boasted to Solon that he was the happiest man alive. Solon replied that people should not be considered to have had happy lives until after they had died, because life can always turn sour. Solon was right. Croesus eventually lost everything. But since Solon probably died before Croesus came to the throne of Lydia, the story is unlikely to be true.

PEISISTRATOS, THE TYRANT

Although Solon reformed the constitution, he could not control what the Athenians did with their new rights. Life was better for the poorest Athenians, but the aristocrats were still behaving arrogantly and competing for power. Because of aristocratic rivalries, the Areopagus was unable to agree on an archon in 590 BCE and again in 586 BCE. The archon chosen for 581 BCE, Damisas, refused to stand down from office at the end of his year and held on to power for an

Peisistratos (602–527 BCE) reigned intermittently as tyrant of Athens from 557 BCE until his death.

extra ten months before being removed. Less than fifteen years after Solon's reforms, it was clear that although the reforms had prevented a mass revolution, they could not protect Athens from ambitious individuals seeking power.

It was not long before what the aristocrats feared actually happened. A prominent aristocrat called Peisistratos, who had been a successful polemarch in the war against Megara, attempted to become tyrant. In 561 BCE Peisistratos entered the marketplace in Athens after inflicting wounds upon himself. He claimed that political enemies had attacked him, and the Athenians gave him a bodyguard, which he then used to take control of the Acropolis. The supporters of two other aristocrats, Lykourgos and Megakles, managed to drive Peisistratos out of Athens. Megakles was the grandson of the earlier Megakles who expelled Kylon.

A few years later, circa 557 BCE, Peisistratos tried again. This time his trick was even more daring. He found a beautiful, 6-foot (182-centimeter) tall woman called Phye and dressed her as the goddess Athena. He started a rumor that the goddess was bringing him back to Athens personally and drove into Athens on a chariot, with Phye beside him. This time Peisistratos had the support of Megakles, whose daughter he was to marry. The Athenians were fooled, and Peisistratos established himself as tyrant. However, the marriage of Peisistratos and Megakles' daughter was not happy, and when she complained to her father he withdrew his support of Peisistratos, who was once more forced to leave Athens.

Peisistratos tried to assume power a third time. He raised a good deal of money and gathered together troops with the help of his friends in other poleis. After a ten-year absence, in 546 BCE he arrived in Attica at the head of an army. There was little resistance, and his position as tyrant was secure. This time it was Megakles who had to leave Athens. Peisistratos ruled Athens until his death in 527 BCE. Although he did not officially change the laws or any of the constitutional arrangements of Solon, he did add some new measures of his own, and some of the old laws must have gone out of use. It was at this time that the confusion over which laws were genuinely enacted by Solon began to grow.

ISONOMIA

After the death of Peisistratos, his son Hippias took over as tyrant. Where Peisistratos had been popular, reducing the power of the aristocracy and building many fine temples in Athens, Hippias was very unpopular, and his regime became brutal and violent. An assassination attempt in 514 BCE only managed to kill Hipparkhos, the brother of Hippias. In the end, it required the intervention of Sparta, one of the leading poleis in Greece, to remove Hippias from power in 510 BCE.

The Athenians were determined never to endure the rule of a tyrant again. When Cleisthenes came forward in 508 BCE with a plan to change the constitution, he won great support. Cleisthenes radically changed the political system in Athens. He gave ultimate power to the Ekklesia, an assembly of all male adult Athenian citizens, and set up an executive council to advise the Ekklesia. All members of the assembly could speak and vote in the Ekklesia and could be chosen by lot to serve for one year on the executive council. The right to become magistrates was extended to hippeis and zeugitae, and in practice the thetes were never

This nineteenth-century engraving depicts the assassination of Hipparkhos, brother of Hippias, in 514 BCE.

excluded either. This was power exercised by the people and for the people. Athens had become a democracy. The Athenians did not at this time call their system *demokratia* ("people power"); they called it *isonomia* or "equality in law," something that would not have been possible without Solon's reforms. Cleisthenes did not attempt to make changes to the laws, many of which were still those that Solon had first written down.

SOLON'S INTENTIONS

Solon did not create a democracy in Athens. He was not even trying to do so, as his poetry reveals, "The people will best follow their leaders, / If they are neither too free nor too restricted."

Solon remained an aristocrat at heart and wanted to avoid the overthrow of the ruling class through popular discontent. However, he also worked on the principle of fairness. Solon saw that it was unfair for the poor Athenians who worked hard for the good of the polis to be enslaved, and so he gave them freedom. He saw that it was unfair for those who worked hard to be deprived of political

POWER AND ACCOUNTABILITY

There are two spectrums on which a country's government must reside. One is the percentage, or relative number of citizens who hold power. At one end of that spectrum is democracy, where all people have power and influence. At the other end is absolute monarchy, where a single ruler makes decisions for everyone. Anarchy is one step beyond absolute monarchy, but doesn't fit onto this spectrum because in anarchy there is no government at all.

The other spectrum is the accountability of rulers. At one end, rulers must give all consideration to the needs of their constituents or they risk losing power by losing an election or by being convicted of corruption. At the other end of this spectrum, rulers work to preserve only their rule or whatever self-serving interest they care about, and it is impossible to hold them accountable for their actions, especially without dissolving the government itself. But a particularly deceitful corrupt official in a society of accountability can avoid detection for a long time, and a change in regime opens space for dissent and resistance.

A single country's government eventually slides to different parts of these spectrums.

rights, and so he gave them their chance by changing from a system based on birth to one based on wealth. Solon thought it was fair that those who owned most of the land and wealth should have control over that land and wealth, so he left power in the hands of the rich. He also realized that it was fair for the poor to be free from exploitation, so he wrote down the laws to protect them.

The principle of the rule of law is central to any democracy. It means that members of the democracy can know and enforce their rights. The rule of law means that the laws overrule the will of any individual leader, and that the leader must obey the laws as much as any other citizen. Solon established the rule of law at Athens with his eunomia.

Although Solon achieved his short-term goal of avoiding an immediate political crisis, in the long term his reforms were a failure because the established order was overthrown when Peisistratos became tyrant of Athens. However, by the fourth century BCE, the Athenians remembered Solon as the "father of democracy" because they still had the laws he had written down. They also knew that he had given freedom to the poorest Athenians, which was a necessary first step before Cleisthenes gave them political rights.

This plaster bust made by Anna Christoforidis in 2004 re-creates the supposed image of Cleisthenes.

Some nations today have democratic political systems because the Athenians had it. When people during the Renaissance studied the literature and philosophy of the Athenians, they also studied the Athenian political system, and that system was democracy. Just as intellectuals tried to copy the literature, they also aimed to imitate the political system, and this gave rise to modern democracy. Solon made Athenian democracy possible, and so he also made later democracies possible, including that of the United States. His contributions are remembered to this day.

THE PROBLEM OF EVIDENCE

There are few precise details about Solon, but even a known fact can have many interpretations or its significance can be unclear. This is because no one wrote down the events that happened during Solon's reign, or if someone did, that record is lost. The very first known book about history was not written until about 530 BCE. After this time, the Athenians did try to write about the life and times of Solon, but they did not have a written record of what he had done. They had some pieces of the poems attributed to

Solon, some laws that Solon was credited with enacting, and they had oral traditions, stories passed on from parents to children.

Although oral traditions can be very reliable, there is the risk that the storyteller wants to spin a good story and is not concerned with the truth. By the time a story has been passed down through a couple of generations, it is sometimes impossible to say which parts of the story are true and which are made up. So when the Athenians finally wrote about Solon, it was as if they had only half the pieces of a jigsaw puzzle. But they did their best to make sense of what they knew and to imagine what the whole picture would have looked like.

Only a few of the books that the ancient Athenians wrote survive. Earlier Athenians could look at dozens of poems and choose which ones to quote, but modern historians have only the lines of poetry recorded in those later works. The ancients could look at all the laws that Solon was said to have made and choose the ones they thought were genuine. Contemporary scholars have only the laws the ancients selected. And the same is true of the oral tradition. If the early Athenians who followed Solon got it wrong, then there is little chance today that we can get it right. It is clear that the ancients did not always get it right because sometimes they disagreed with each other. At other times it is clear that they are only guessing, because what they say is deliberately vague.

Of the many books that the Greeks wrote about Solon, only two have survived. One, known as the *Constitution of Athens*, was written by Aristotle in circa 335 BCE. Aristotle was a philosopher who was interested in how human society worked. He collected information about many different Greek poleis, one of which was Athens. Because he was writing about the history of the constitution of Athens, he would have tried to get information that was as accurate as possible. However, since the book is not just about Solon, the section devoted to his achievements is not very detailed.

The other book is the *Life of Solon* by Plutarch, written circa 100 CE, which is about seven hundred years after the events he describes.

Sculpture of Aristotle, ancient philosopher and author of the *Constitution of Athens*.

Because it was written so long after Solon, the book is much more confusing than the *Constitution of Athens* by Aristotle. It is much longer, however, because it is only about Solon. It also describes Solon himself, not just what he did. The problem is that most of the stories Plutarch provides about Solon are from the oral tradition and are not reliable.

These two writers cite many quotations from the poems of Solon. There are also many other writers who quoted from Solon's poems, even if they were not writing about Solon himself. Some of these are lawyers, who wrote down the speeches they made in court to help train their students. Because Solon wrote many of the laws of Athens, they sometimes mention him.

Today, when historians try to sort out what Solon really did and what is simply fiction, they compare all the different pieces of information that are available. Sometimes one ancient writer tells a story about Solon and a different ancient writer tells the exact story about someone else. This often means that the story is true about the person who lived first, although sometimes it is clearly not

This engraving depicts Plutarch, an ancient Greek essayist and biographer who created such noteable works as *Life of Solon*.

true about either. For example, the ancient writers believed that Solon changed the coins of Athens. But archaeology tells us that Athens did not have coins until after Solon was archon, so he could not have changed them.

By testing evidence in this way, historians can create theories about what is presumed to be true. Unfortunately, there is no guarantee that the details are correct. Sometimes a conclusion is simply a guess.

acropolis A hill that the Greeks built most of their cities on or around that was easy to defend from enemies; the most famous acropolis is the Acropolis of Athens.

archon Potentially anyone who was in charge of something, but it usually means someone with an official government position; at Athens, the most senior magistrate.

Areopagus A small hill in Athens, sacred to Ares, the god of war, where the aristocratic council met; more commonly used as the name of the council itself.

Attica The name given to the geographical region surrounding the polis of Athens.

demokratia The system of direct rule of a polis by all the citizens, meeting in the Ekklesia.

Ekklesia The name of the assembly of all citizens at Athens, which met for one day approximately forty times each year, to decide policies and to pass laws.

eunomia The principle that society should be balanced, with no one group having more power than they deserved.

hektemoroi A group of Athenians who worked on farms for either one sixth of what they produced or who were required to pay only one sixth of what they produced to the landowners.

Heliaia The name given to the court of all adult male Athenians, which Solon established to hear appeals against the decisions of magistrates.

hippeis Horsemen. The name of Solon's class whose land produced enough for them to be able to maintain a horse and fight in the cavalry.

horoi Freestanding stones inscribed with the name of the owner of the land as a marker.

isonomia The principle that all citizens had a right to equal treatment under the law.

magistrate An individual with an official government position (called a magistracy), who had legal powers to act as a judge and, to some extent, to make new laws for a specific area of law.

medimnoi Those whose land produced 500 or more bushels of grain (a bushel being about 8 gallons [30 liters], and 500 bushels of barley weighing over 15 tons).

medimnos A bushel. A Greek measure of capacity, roughly equal to 8 gallons (30 liters) , that was used to measure dry produce such as grain or flour.

nomoi Unwritten customs or written laws.

oracle The name given to any of the places where the Greeks believed they could go and get advice directly from the gods; the term used for the piece of advice given from the Delphic priestess when Apollo spoke through her.

polemarch The title of the magistrate at Athens who was responsible for the army.

polis A Greek city-state.

sanctuary The area surrounding every Greek temple that was marked by a wall and offered refuge to people who had committed a crime.

seisachtheia The name of Solon's cancellation of debts, which included setting debt-slaves free and abolishing hektemoroi.

thetes Day laborers, the lowest of Solon's classes. It included all those who were too poor to possess their own pair of oxen and owned very small farms or no land at all.

tyrant Someone who took power in a polis by means that ignored the constitution and ruled as an individual.

zeugitae The third of Solon's classes, whose land produced enough for them to keep a pair of oxen of their own and who would be wealthy enough to pay for the armor to fight in the infantry.

American Classical League
Miami University
Oxford, OH 45056
(513) 529-7741
Website: http://www.aclclassics.org

This organization supports the study of classical languages, including Greek, and offers materials and job search help for those who need it.

Association of Ancient Historians
Denise Demetriou
University of California, San Diego
Department of History, Mail Code 0104
Humanities and Social Sciences Building Rm 4047
9500 Gilman Drive
La Jolla, CA 92093-0104
Website: http://associationofancienthistorians.org/index.html

This membership association supports ancient history professionals by planning annual meetings where scholars can present the latest in research and find resources that can connect them to other scholars.

Canadian Museum of History
100 Laurier Street
Gatineau, QC K1A 0M8
Canada
(800) 555-5621

Website: http://www.historymuseum.ca/

This museum offers exhibits, activities, and artifacts to allow the public to engage with and learn about ancient and more recent history.

International Plutarch Society
Ploutarchos,
Department of History
Utah State University
0710 Old Main Hill
Logan, UT 84322-0710
Website: http://ips.ploutarchos.org

This membership society offers information about conferences, publications, and news relevant to scholars of Plutarch.

Museum of Classical Antiquities
Desmarais Building
55 Laurier Avenue East, 3th Floor
Ottawa, ON K1N 6N5
Canada
(613) 562-5800
Website: https://arts.uottawa.ca/cla-srs/en/museum

Located at the University of Ottawa, this museum offers workshops and guided tours and hands-on learning via activities and exercises that are meant to help participants gain a greater understanding of ancient Greece and Rome.

National Junior Classical League
Miami University
Oxford, OH 45056-1694
(513) 529-7741
Website: http://www.njcl.org

This national organization promotes the study of ancient Greek and Roman life. It offers contests, test preparation, and other ways for members to engage.

WEBSITES

Because of the changing nature of internet links, Rosen Publishing has developed an online list of websites related to the subject of this book. This site is updated regularly. Please use this link to access the list:

http://www.rosenlinks.com/LANW/solon

FOR FURTHER READING

Balot, Ryan K., ed. *A Companion to Greek and Roman Political Thought*. Hoboken, NJ: Wiley-Blackwell, 2012.

Bernardete, Seth. *Herodotean Inquiries*. South Bend, IN: St. Augustine's Press, 2009.

Ehrenberg, Victor. *From Solon to Socrates: Greek History and Civilisation During the 6th and 5th Centuries BC*. London, UK: Routledge, 2014.

Kuiper, Kathleen. *Ancient Greece* (The Britannica Guide to Ancient Civilizations). New York, NY: Brittanica Educational Publishing, 2011.

Lefkowitz, Mary R. *The Lives of the Greek Poets*. London, UK: Bloomsbury, 2013.

Lewis, John David. *Solon the Thinker: Political Thought in Archaic Athens*. London, UK: Bloomsbury Publishing, 2013.

Morgan, Kathryn A., ed. *Popular Tyranny: Sovereignty and Its Discontents in Ancient Greece*. Austin, TX: University of Texas Press, 2013.

Sanders, Lionel Jehuda. *Dionysius I of Syracuse and Greek Tyranny* (Routledge Revivals). London, UK: Routledge, 2014.

Stafford, Emma. *Exploring the Life, Myth, and Art of Ancient Greece* (Civilizations of the World). New York, NY: Rosen Publishing, 2012.

Teegarden, David. *Death to Tyrants!: Ancient Greek Democracy and the Struggle against Tyranny*. Princeton, NJ: Princeton University Press, 2013.

Adams, John Paul. "Solon of Athens." California State University, Northridge, August 8, 2001. https://www.csun.edu/~hcfll004/solon.html.

Alverno College. "Types of Governments." Retrieved November 17, 2016. http://depts.alverno.edu/dgp/GEC/Types%20of%20Government.html.

Cammack, Daniela Louise. "Rethinking Athenian Democracy." Doctor of Philosophy dissertation, Harvard University, Janauary 2013. http://nrs.harvard.edu/urn-3:HUL.InstRepos:10423842.

Copeland, Tim. *Ancient Greece*. New York, NY: Cambridge University Press, 1997.

Diamond, Larry. "What is Democracy?" Lecture at Hilla University for Humanistic Studies. January 21, 2004. https://web.stanford.edu/~ldiamond/iraq/WhaIsDemocracy012004.htm.

Dunstan, William. *Ancient Greece*. Fort Worth, TX: Harcourt College Publishers, 2000.

Freeman, Kathleen. *The Work and Life of Solon*. New York, NY: Arno Press, 1976.

Harris, Kenton. "Distributive Jusitice." Florida International University, April 11, 2012. http://www2.fiu.edu/~harrisk/Notes/Ethics/Distributive%20Jusitice.htm.

Leggett, Brian. "Solon: The Art of Knowing." Blog Network. IESE Business School University of Navarra, December 6, 2012. http://blog

.iese.edu/leggett/2012/06/12/solon-the-art-of-knowing.

Marmorstein, Art. "The Rise of Athens (Part II--Pisistratos to Cleisthenes)." Northern State University, 2015. www3.northern.edu/marmorsa/AthensLecturePartII.htm.

Mitchell, Lynette, and Rhodes, Peter. *The Development of the Polis in Archaic Greece*. London, UK: Routledge, 1997.

Ortencio Flores, Samuel. "The Roles of Solon in Plato's Dialogues." Doctor of Philosophy dissertation. Ohio State University, 2013. https://etd.ohiolink.edu/!etd.send_file?accession=osu1371638577&disposition=inline

Perseus Project. "Frequently Asked Questions about the Ancient Olympic Games." Tufts University, August 13, 2004. http://www.perseus.tufts.edu/Olympics/faq1.html.

Thiel, Johannes Hendrik. *Studies in Ancient History*. Amsterdam, Netherlands: J. C. Gieben, 1994.

Woodhouse, W. *Solon the Liberator*. London, UK: Oxford University Press, 1938.

ABOUT THE AUTHORS

Beatriz Santillian earned her BA in English in 2003 and her PhD in history in 2009. She is a fan of all things to do with ancient history and loves to learn about artifacts from the past. Santillian writes on topics concerning culture, technology, and change, and she also writes software in her spare time. She lives in Rochester, New York, with her daughter.

Bernard Randall read ancient history and philosophy at St. Andrew's University, Scotland, before moving to the University of Edinburgh, Scotland, for a master's degree in classics. He completed his doctorate on fifth century BCE Greece at the University of Manchester England. He has taught Greek and Roman history at the University of Manchester, and Greek history for the Open University. His main research interest is the history of Sparta to 400 BCE. His other interests include early church history and theology, rugby, the Discworld novels of Terry Pratchett, and juggling.

PHOTO CREDITS

Cover, p. 3 DEA/L. Pedicini/De Agostini/Getty Images; cover (background) Print Collector/Hulton Fine Art Collection/Getty Images; pp. 6–7 milosk50/Shutterstock.com; pp. 12–13 De Agostini Picture Library/Getty Images; p. 14 ZU_09/E+/Getty Images; pp. 16–17 Ivan Vdovin/Alamy Stock Photo; pp. 20–21 Private Collection/© Look and Learn/Bridgeman Images; pp. 24–25 Mansell/The LIFE Picture Collection/Getty Images; pp. 28, 62–63, 84 Interfoto/Alamy Stock Photo; pp. 30–31 Bildagentur-online/Universal Images Group/Getty Images; pp. 34, 40, 98 Bettmann/Getty Images; pp. 37, 67, 82 DEA/G. Dagli Orti/De Agostini/Getty Images; pp. 42–43 Stefano Bianchetti/Corbis Historical/Getty Images; p. 46 Leemage/Corbis Historical/Getty Images; p. 48 mango-two-friendly/Shutterstock.com; p. 51 19th era 2/Alamy Stock Photo; p. 53 © iStockphoto.com/Kenneth Wiedemann; p. 58 Erin Babnik/Alamy Stock Photo; p. 70 Chronicle/Alamy Stock Photo; pp. 78–79 National Geographic Creative/Bridgeman Images; p. 88 PHAS/Universal Images Group/Getty Images; p. 92 Pictures from History/Bridgeman Images; p. 96 MidoSemsem/Shutterstock.com; interior pages background images © iStockphoto.com/kikkalek5050 (sky), Triff/Shutterstock.com (map).

Designer: Brian Garvey; Editor: Bernadette Davis; Photo Researcher: Karen Huang